The Fairytale Hairdresser

and

BEAUTY AND THE BEAST

Abie Longstaff
&
Lauren Beard

PICTURE CORGI

Kittie Lacey was the best hairdresser in all the land.

This week her salon was busier than ever! Princess Cinderella and Prince Charming were planning a birthday ball for their baby boy and everyone wanted to look beautiful.

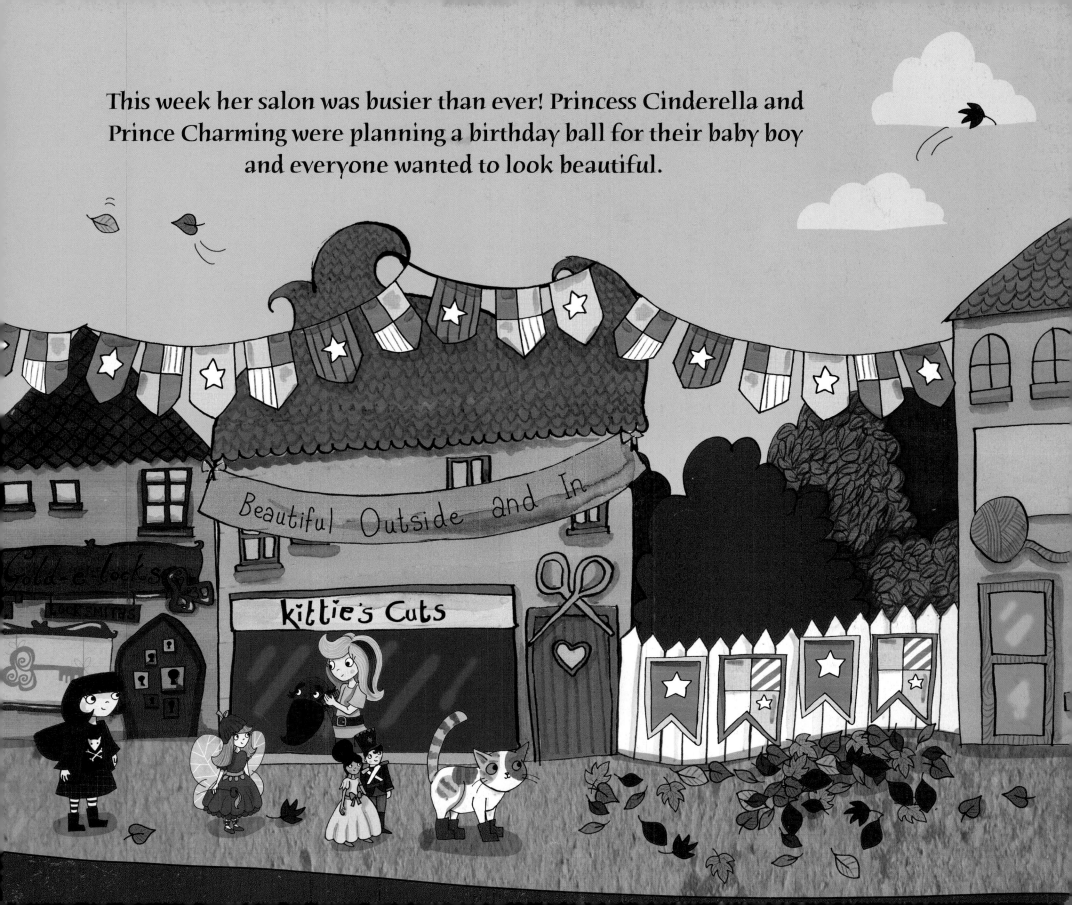

Kittie had been working so hard! She really needed a rest, so she closed the salon early and went for a picnic with her friend Bella, the most beautiful girl in Fairyland.

Bella was a painter and the official artist for the royal ball.
While Bella painted, Kittie practised hairstyles.

Suddenly there was a mighty thunderclap and rain began to pour down.
"Oh no!" cried Bella. "My paintings will be ruined!"

Kittie had an idea. "Let's go to Beast's castle. He'll give us shelter."
Bella was frightened – she had heard that Beast was mean and scary.

The castle door swung open and there stood Beast. He was tall and hairy, with big ears and huge paws. "Come in," he growled.

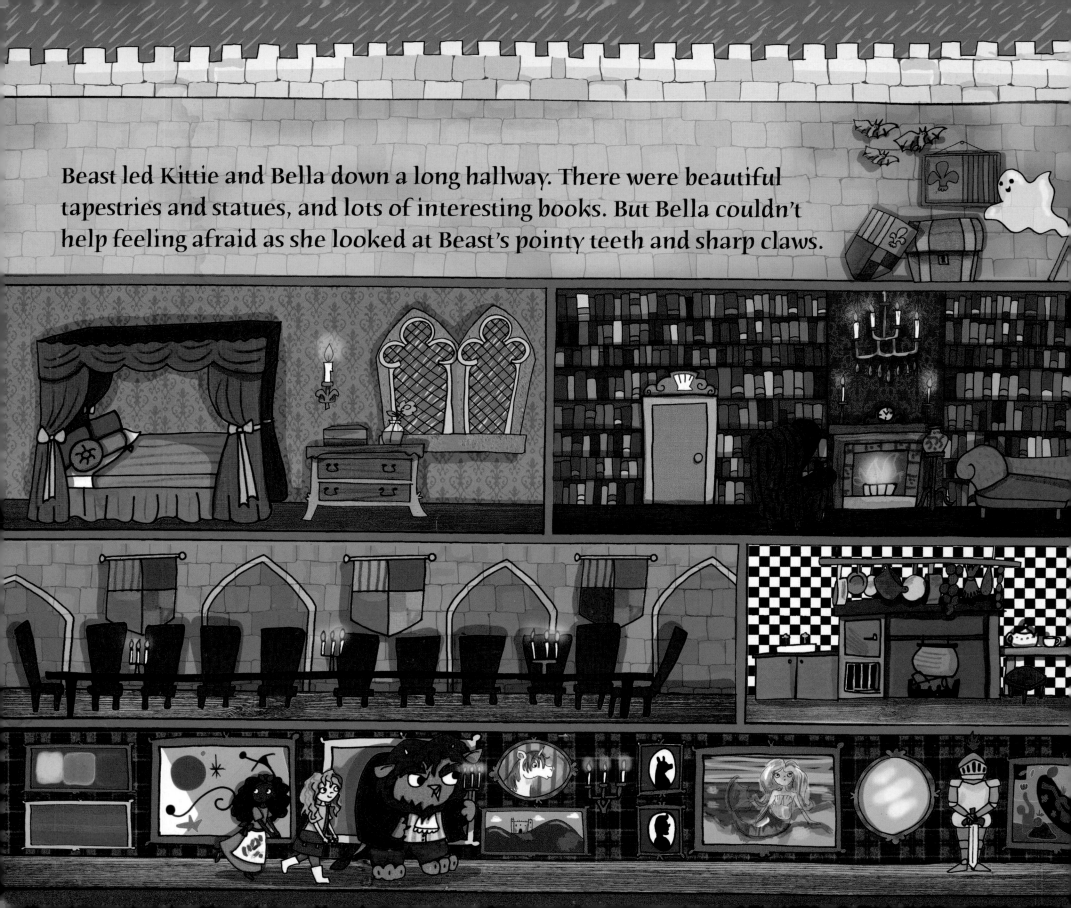

Beast led Kittie and Bella down a long hallway. There were beautiful tapestries and statues, and lots of interesting books. But Bella couldn't help feeling afraid as she looked at Beast's pointy teeth and sharp claws.

A gong sounded. **Bong!**
"It's time for dinner," Beast growled.

Bella was amazed to see a delicious meal set out in the elegant dining room. Over dinner Bella and Beast talked and talked about art and music and books. Bella soon realised that Beast wasn't mean – he was just a bit shy.

Kittie smiled to herself – her two friends were getting on very well!

Later, by the fire, Bella took out her sketchpad and began a portrait of Beast. She sketched for many hours, until the rain stopped.

"I'll come back and finish your picture as soon as I can," Bella promised as she and Kittie made their way home.

The days flew quickly by. The salon was filled with customers asking for:

STRAIGHT hair,

curly hair,

hair **up**,

hair down,

ribbons,

shells,

and a little trim.

On the day of the ball, Kittie was just getting ready when Beast came in looking very unhappy.

"Bella hasn't come back to see me," he said sadly.

"Don't worry, love," said Kittie. "Bella has been busy painting for the ball tonight."

Beast shook his head in despair. "Kittie, do you think Bella could ever love a beast like me?"

"Bella will like you for your heart," said Kittie. "Just be yourself."

"But that's the problem!" cried Beast. "I'm not myself at all!"

Kittie listened as Beast told her his story.

A long time ago, I used to be a prince. My name was Beau and I was famed throughout the land for my handsome face.

Nice times

BEAU, No.1 MOST HANDSOME PRINCE

In those days the castle was filled with people and light, and fun and laughter. But one snowy night a woman came to my door wanting shelter. She was old and ugly, and I was young and vain. I wouldn't let her in.

She cursed me and turned me into a hideous beast! My hands turned to paws, fur covered my body, and my hair grew wild and messy.

"Now Bella will never love me!" Beast howled. "I wish I could be a prince again."

Kittie patted Beast's shoulder. "I can't make you a prince," she said. "But I can make you a bit neater, if you like. Then we can go to the party and see Bella."

Kittie carefully untangled Beast's fur.

And gave it a good wash.

She dried him off,

and styled him.

Finally he was ready and they went to the party together, arm in arm.

Kittie and Beast arrived in the great hall just in time to see Bella present her painting.

But the royal birthday boy was missing. Where had he gone?

Suddenly gasps came from around the ballroom. The baby prince
had climbed up the curtains and was dangling from a chandelier!
The chandelier broke away from the ceiling and began to fall!
"My baby!" cried Cinderella.

Beast sprang
into action:

diving to the floor,
he caught the baby in his
strong paws.

The royal baby was saved . . .
But Beast was hurt!

Bella rushed to his side.
"Oh, Beast!" she sobbed. "Please wake up!"
With her heart breaking, Bella kissed his fur.

There was a bright flash of light and a swirl of magic.

Everyone gasped. In Beast's place stood a handsome man!

"I am Prince Beau," said the man, bowing to Bella.
"Thank you for breaking the curse."
At first Bella was surprised. Where had her Beast gone?

But when she looked into the prince's eyes she recognised her friend.
"It's you!" Bella cried happily.

"I'll never be beastly again," Beau promised. "I'm glad I'm human now, but
I don't want to go back to being a pompous prince. I think I need a new look."
"I can help with that," said Kittie.

Kittie tried lots
of different styles
on Prince Beau,
and before long
they found just
the right one.

"Thank you, Kittie!"

The prince smiled at his
wild new look.

Many weeks later, everybody in Fairyland received special invitations to the wedding of Bella and Prince Beau.

Everyone had a wonderful time.

And Bella and Beau gave a beautiful present
to their best friend, Kittie Lacey.